TEAM TAEKW

3

HOW TO BE CHEERI

D0462656

WITHDRAWN

Master Taekwon Lee & Jeffrey Nodelman

Illustrated by Ethen Beavers

RODALE KIDS

This is a work of fiction. Names, characters, places, and incidents either are the product of the author's imagination or are used fictitiously. Any resemblance to actual persons, living or dead, events, or locales is entirely coincidental.

Copyright © 2019 by ATA International.

All rights reserved. Published in the United States by Rodale Kids, an imprint of Random House Children's Books, a division of Penguin Random House LLC, New York.

Rodale and colophon are registered trademarks and Rodale Kids is a trademark of Penguin Random House LLC.

Visit us on the Web! rhcbooks.com

Educators and librarians, for a variety of teaching tools, visit us at RHTeachersLibrarians.com

Library of Congress Cataloging-in-Publication Data is available upon request.

ISBN 978-1-62336-950-7 (hardcover)
ISBN 978-1-62336-948-4 (trade)
ISBN 978-1-62336-949-1 (ebook)

MANUFACTURED IN CHINA

10 9 8 7 6 5 4 3 2 1

First Edition
Random House Children's Books supports the First Amendment and celebrates the right to read.

CHAPTER 1
THE SUN RISES TO START A BEAUTIFUL DAY, DEEP IN THE WOODS . . .

Aaahhhh, ready to begin the day . . . ten minutes ahead of schedule.
Good morning, Mother and Father! I am ready to seize the day!
You love Saturdays . . .
I'm off to Team Taekwondo Class! Better leave now so I am on time.
Your class doesn't begin for another hour! Why are you always so early?
I have team synch demo practice today. It's very important . . . Plus, early is on time. On time is late. And late is unacceptable!

Wake up, Baeoh! You're late . . . again!
Just five more minutes . . .
If you ever want to gain respect from your teammates, you need to be on time for practice.
Practice? Is it Saturday again? Can I have more milk?
Class starts in five minutes! You're gonna be late!
I still have five minutes? Oh boy, I should swing by the playground!
It takes you ten minutes to get there! No playground!

Let's begin . . .
Charyeout . . .
Kyung nae!
Whew! I knew I would make it! I still had time to stop by the playground . . .
BAEOH! You are late . . . again!
Sorry, sir. Permission to join class?

This is your sixth time being late this week.
I know, sir. My dog ate my . . . breakfast.
You don't have a dog. And what's that in your hand?
Oh, there's my breakfast! Yum!
Don't worry, sir, I know what to do next time.
Ride the slide . . . it's way faster than the swings!
Baeoh, it's not what you know that's important. It's what you do.
Huh?
Respect is not what you know . . .
. . . IT'S WHAT YOU DO, SIR!
Next week at testing, you will perform a team synchronized demo.

Remember, class, learning to work as a team is very important.
Teamwork teaches us to respect others through trust, care, and courtesy.
Mir, you brought the most buddies to class last week. We will be a team. Everyone else, read the scroll on the wall to see who your teammate is.
Master Jahngsoo & Mir
Ara & Raon
Narsha & Baron
Choa & Suri
Baeoh & Cheeri

Class, pair up with your teammate and remember... respect is not what you know...
...IT'S WHAT YOU DO, SIR!!!
I LOVE team sync demos!

WE ARE...
TEAM PRIDE!

WE...
ARE...
TEAM EXCELLENCE!

WE ARE TEAM SOAR!

WE ARE TEAM...
BUUUURRRRPR!!

Baeoh! Remember, if you want to gain respect, you must have good manners and courtesy.
Excuse me, sir.

You'd better take this seriously. I have a perfect score on all my tests. Don't mess that up!
I have matching costumes! We'll be team FUN! Who can mess that up?
First team exercise—mirror techniques. Stay together as a team!

Side kick for ten seconds!
One . . . two . . . three . . . four . . .
성
five . . . six . . . seven . . . eight . . .
성
. . . don't you dare drop that leg . . .
Uggggh . . .
. . . nine . . . ten.
성
Next drill.
Baeoh, this
time you pick.

Yes! My turn!
Cheeri, let's do this!
I don't think so.
You must learn to work together. Listen to each other and learn to trust.
We are Team Perfection. Our demo must be perfect.
To be perfect, we need to have fun and enjoy ourselves.
To be perfect, we need to BE perfect. Meet me an hour before class to practice tomorrow.

CHAPTER 2
성
실
Respect is not what you know, it's what you do.

You're late . . . as usual.
Sorry, I got distracted.
The slide?
No. I would have been on time, but I saw this caterpillar and wanted to watch it turn into a butterfly.

Did it turn into a butterfly?
Well ... er ... no. Not yet ...
Then why were you late?
I was encouraging it and cheering it on!
Well, maybe tomorrow. He KNOWS what to do ... he just needs to DO! Mad RESPECT for that caterpillar!

Okay . . . we have lots to cover today, and unless we get started, this day will never end.
Okay . . .
I worked ahead and made some notes.
TEAM FUN PERFECTION

Okay, before we can synchronize, we need to figure out what we can both do with perfection.
TEAM FUN PERFECTION
I hope this involves eating...
grumble!
I'll go first.

That was awesome!
The way you did the thing ... with the jumping thingy ... and double kicky thing-a-ma-jiggy ... in the air!
And the fierce face you made in that fighting stance ... so cool! I didn't know you could do that!

CHAPTER 3
Thanks. What can you do?
Oh, none of that . . .
Well, I have been working on my 1080 kick! Check it out!
AAAAAAAAAA!!
THUD!
Still working on that one . . .

You can't even do a 540, but you want to do a 1080? It's twice as hard!
No it isn't! It's still only one jump with the same kick.
It's twice the kick . . . do the math.
Uhhhh, I don't think I can. Not enough fingers!

I like how it feels when I'm jumping and spinning in the air!
What's the point when you don't have any control?
What's the fun in jumping with control?

You can't plan *everything*.
SOME...
TIMES...
YOU...
JUST...
HAVE...
TO...
JUMP!

What are you doing?
I knew this would happen.
TEAM FUN
WHAT TO DO WHEN...
#87
BAEOH JUMPS AROUND LIKE A GOOFBALL AND LOSES CONTROL
199

Okay, time to get serious!
"GET" serious? What have you been so far?!
You never take anything seriously!

How do you expect to pass this test if you cannot take this seriously?
Why do you even do Taekwondo if you don't have any fun while you're doing it?
What do you know about Taekwondo? You don't even know the difference between a 540 kick and a 1080 kick!
It's twice as many spins before you kick!

GROWL
Why do I even bother?
Dude! You could definitely use some self-control! Or a hot dog . . .
Yes! Time for a hot dog!

CHAPTER
4

Cheeri, how can
I help you?

Sorry, Master Jahngsoo. I didn't mean to interrupt you.
Not a problem, young cheetah. Have a seat. What brings you in today?
Well, sir, I'm having some challenges with my teammate. It's hard for me to find respect for him.
Before you can find respect, you must first be respectful.
Wait, I think I'm a little lost . . .

When you lose ground, it is best to find your center. Sit next to me, close your eyes, and breathe . . .

CRASHHHH!!!
Meditation is over.

Excuse me, sir. I don't mean to interrupt, but it's me, Baeoh.
Yes, Baeoh. I know it's you.
CRASH!
That thing looks pretty old . . . you may want to get a new one.

Baeoh, that is a very complex instrument. I will put it back together later. Come, have a seat next to Cheeri.
What is it that brings you here today?
Cheeri and I are having a hard time being on the same team.
Why do you find it difficult being on the same team?
She takes things too seriously.
He doesn't take anything seriously.

Okay. Cheeri, let's start with you.

Sir, I have passed my tests with perfect scores all year! I can't afford to score anything less than perfect.

Sir, I am perfectly happy with my performances all year! I'm getting max stressed trying to be her little "Mr. Perfect"!

Baeoh is constantly joking around. He loves hot dogs ... and he can't tell the difference between 540 and 1080!

Cheeri has a book full of rules! She knows what to do when I do my happy-jumpy dance. And she did so many jumpy-kicky thingies today that I lost count... And it's 540!

540? What does that mean?
He means the difference between a 540 and a 1080.
Thank you, ...I think.
Well, I accept one thing very clearly. Each of you is very confident with yourself.
Now you must learn to accept. You must learn to walk in each other's shoes.
Is Cheeri giving me her shoes?
Baeoh has shoes? I bet they are stinky...
Heeeey!

Acceptance is allowing others to be themselves. If you are to walk in each other's shoes, you will learn to accept each other.
Cheeri, what do you enjoy about yourself?
I like being organized . . . I can find everything when I want it! I feel strongest when I am prepared for every test!
Good. Baeoh, what do you enjoy about yourself?
I like to laugh. I like to make others laugh! It makes me laugh, and I feel good inside. When I feel good inside . . . I laugh!
And hot dogs! I love those, too!

The two of you are so different. You couldn't be any further from each other.
You are . . . the PERFECT TEAM.
Huh?
You must learn to work together. The only way you can learn from each other is to walk in each other's shoes. If you do so, you will know what it is like to be each other.
Again with the shoes? Are we going somewhere?

But isn't self-esteem the joy of being myself?
Yes. But in order to respect others, you must accept who they are and learn what it is like to be them.
You must "walk in their shoes."

Ooooh. I think it's beginning to make sense.
Yeaaah . . .
The fog is being lifted from the flip-flops of my mind . . .

Cheeri, Baeoh, it is time that you both experience each other's life in order to appreciate and accept it.
Do you accept the challenge?
Yes, sir!
What size shoe do you wear? Four? Maybe a five?

CHAPTER
5

CLICK!

Baeoh, why are you here so early? Class doesn't start for another two hours.
I'm not me, sir. I'm Cheeri.
You are... Cheeri?
I mean, I'm me! I'm acting like Cheeri, but I'm still me. A boy cub, you know...
Here on time, sir!
Okay...?

Good morning!
Hey, Ara! What's up, dude?!
Not much! Ugh . . .
Hello! Yes it is!
Can't wait to see Baeoh and Cheeri's demo!
Should be . . . interesting.

Dude, check it out! Baeoh's early.
And practicing his form?
What's going on?
Yeah, where's Cheeri?
Hello, ma'am! Hello, sir!
Who are you? And what have you done with Baeoh?
Class! Line up!

Charyeout!
Kyung nae!
You're late! Everything okay?
I have a bellyache.

I think I had one too many hot dogs...
BURRP!
Aaaah, bellyache...gone!
Baeoh!... I mean, Cheeri, if you want to gain respect of others, you must practice courtesy and good manners.
Yes, sir. Excuse me.

Face your partner...
Time to begin jump side
kicks on the target!
Begin!
Dude! When did
you learn to kick
so strong?!
HIYAH!
Woah

Class, switch! Begin!
You can do this, Raon! Jump high and kick strong!
Suri, are we doing this, or what?
Where'd you go?
Oh, there you are. Sorry, I didn't see you down there...
Because you're so short! Buahahaha!

You can do this, Raon! Your last kick was awesome!
Uh . . . thanks?
Baeoh, what's gotten into you?
Let me see your best kick!
Hey, Cheeri, did you hit your head or something?
Too . . . many . . . hot dogs . . .
Did someone say . . . . hot dogs?
Face your partner! Charyeout, Kyung nae!
Class, stack up the kicking shields. Dismissed.

Okay, let's bring them in, nice and neat.
Keep them straight! One at a time!
Good! One more before we start the next stack!
Let's start the next stack!

Very nicely done, class! Remember, there's no "I" in "team"...
But there's M-E!
ME! You get it?
Okay, you two. We got this...whoever you are...

Hey, guys, see you tomorrow.
Yeah, see you next time . . .

Boy, being you makes me . . .
. . . sick to my stomach . . . I may hurl . . .
Did you save me a hot dog?
Dude, I ate them all. That's why I was late.
I can't feel my . . . anything . . . did you just call me dude?
Okay . . . Good luck with practice.

Good bye . . . sir?
He's already gone.
WHEEEW!
I think I could pass out for a week!

I am so tired. I didn't think it was possible to be this tired.
How do you eat so many hot dogs?
I think I'm going to explode!
Oh, a hot dog would be so awesome right now . . .

Except . . . I'm too tired to chew.
You could use a blender!

HAHAHAHA
You know, when you want, you can be pretty funny!
RUMBLE
Buahahaha!
HAHAHAHAHAHAHAHAHA

I saw you do a couple of really nice kicks when you were focused!
Who, me? Oh, thanks . . .
Honestly, it was hard for me to concentrate so much.
I think I broke my brain . . .

It was pretty cool getting a compliment from Raon.
Yeah, your kicks were strong! You almost knocked him over!
You earned his respect for sure!
Really? Wow! I usually have to make them laugh to get any respect.

Yeah, it was pretty fun getting the team to laugh!
But I think we took it a little too far. I owe Suri an apology.
Yes, it's important to still show respect through good manners and courtesy...
...especially when you are having fun.

It's not what you know...
It's what you do!
RESPECT!
I like being me, and I can see what you like about being you.
Wow! Your shoes are comfortable!

Now I know what it's like
to "wear your shoes."
Oh! That's what
Master Jahngsoo
wanted us to learn!
Yeah, but I definitely
cannot walk a mile in
your shoes right now.
Agreed!
Me neither!

So, how do we be ourselves again and figure out how to work together?
You make the plan, and I'll get the sombreros.
Sounds good, except for the hats . . . we can have fun without hats . . .
You're right. Fake mustaches are much better . . .

But first, I vote we lie here for a little bit longer...
I second that vote!
That's twice as many votes...
예
You sure you don't have a hot dog hiding somewhere?
Oh, Baeoh...

TEAM FUN PERFECTION
Okay, Baeoh, so after the introduction, we should start with our first combo, followed by our kick combos.
That sounds great! Maybe we can add a spin kick for the finale!
A spin kick sounds good...
TEAM FUN PERFECTION
...but I think a 1080 kick is even better!
Oh gosh, I haven't been able to land that yet...
Then I believe we'd better start practicing!
Belief is "Yes, I can!"

You just need help focusing.
Here, kick my hand.
RESPECT!

That was an awesome kick!
I can't believe I landed that 1080! Thanks for your help!
Thanks to you, I had a lot of fun, too!
It was my pleasure!
Hey! That's the caterpillar, or *was* the caterpillar! Good for you!
Good for us!

CHAPTER
6

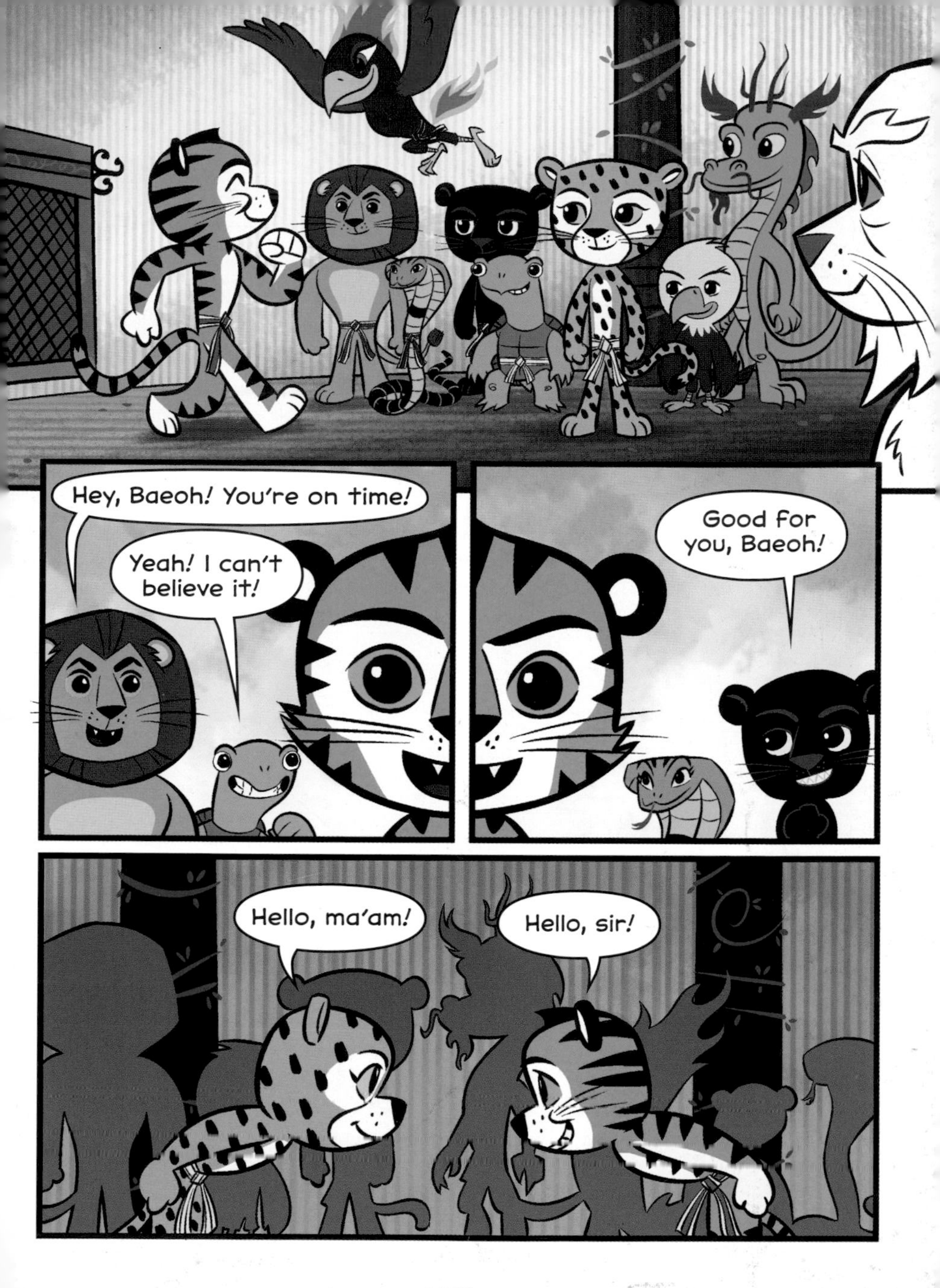
Hey, Baeoh! You're on time!
Yeah! I can't believe it!
Good for you, Baeoh!
Hello, ma'am!
Hello, sir!

Baeoh, you made it!
I knew you would be early!
So did you get in your practice at home?
Yes, a little ... not much ...
No.
WHAT?!

Just kidding.
I did.
Don't worry!
I got this!
And what is that
spot on your chest?
Ha! Made
you look!

HAHA HAHA HA HA HAHAHA
Uh, are you two okay? You don't seem like yourselves . . .
Yup! I'm me again. But part her, too!
But mostly me. I like me!
I like her, too . . . but mostly me.

Umm, okay . . . I think?
What he means is . . . yes, we are just fine!
You see, everyone, Master Jahngsoo pushed us to work together.
We learned to accept each other for who we are.
With a little care and trust, we gained confidence in each other.
We had to listen to each other . . . and practice good manners.
Yes, I'm sorry I was rude to you, Suri. I didn't mean to disrespect you. It just kind of happened . . .
Especially after eating hot dogs.

Everybody, line up!
YES, SIR!
I PROMISE TO BE A GOOD PERSON, WITH KNOWLEDGE IN MY MIND, HONESTY IN MY HEART, STRENGTH IN MY BODY, TO MAKE GOOD FRIENDS, AND . . . I WILL BECOME A BLACK BELT LEADER!
Yes I can!

Time for team sync demos! Mir and I will go first . . .
WE...
ARE...
TEAM...
LEADERSHIP!

예
WE...
ARE...

TEAM...
EXCELLENCE!!!

WE...
ARE...

TEAM...
SOAR!

ROAR!
WE...
ARE...

TEAM...
AWESOME!
Oh boy, glad that's over with!

We have traditional music with our demo, sir!
May we begin?
Permission granted!
Hit play. When I tell you, change the music to this.
You got it, Baeoh. Good luck!
Ahh, this music is beautiful. The sound of the flute reminds me of my home.

NOW!

Ready?
I was born ready!
WE...
ARE...
TEAM...
PER-FUN-CTION!

WOOHOO!
WOOT!
YEAH!
It is clear who the winners are. You have earned respect from each other, and most importantly, from yourselves.
I didn't think I was going to pull off the first part of the demo!
And I thought I was going to be embarrassed in the second half!
I like being me with you!
Me too! Let's get a hot dog to celebrate!
I respect that idea!

I PROMISE:

TO BE A GOOD PERSON,
WITH KNOWLEDGE IN MY MIND,
HONESTY IN MY HEART,
STRENGTH IN MY BODY,
TO MAKE GOOD FRIENDS,
AND...
I WILL BECOME
A BLACK BELT LEADER!

ARA (A-RA)

Ara is a shy turtle. Before joining Team Taekwondo, he usually just stayed in his shell. Now he is making new friends and loves to do his forms nice and slow.

Name means: "of the sea"

Belt rank: white

Favorite move: knife hand strike

BAEOH (BAY-OH)

Baeoh is the funniest tiger ever. He has a big heart and loves to laugh. He is everyone's friend but sometimes lacks confidence.

Name means: "flying tiger"

Belt rank: orange

Favorite move: side kick

CHEERI (CHEER-Y)

Cheeri is the hardest worker in the class. Even though she always makes straight A's, she is always trying hard to get better, maybe sometimes too hard.

Name means: "to defend"

Belt rank: yellow

Favorite move: round kick

RAON (RAY-ON)

Raon is the biggest member of Team Taekwondo. He is very strong and a great athlete. Although he always means well, sometimes he leaps before he looks.

Name means: "lion"

Belt rank: camo

Favorite move: reverse punch

SURI (SUR-Y)

Suri comes from a big family of big eagles. He is small for his age and sometimes tries to act bigger than he really is. He always goes too fast but is working on slowing down.

Name means: "eagle"

Belt rank: green

Favorite move: jump front kick

CHOA (CHO-AH)

Choa is a rare phoenix. She is very pretty and likes it when the other animals do things for her. She is learning to do things for herself, and when she does, she is awesome.

Name means: "light of the world"

Belt rank: purple

Favorite move: double knife hand block

MIR (MEER)

Mir is a super smart dragon. He might not be the most coordinated, but he tries really hard. He is learning to control his strength.

Name means: "dragon"

Belt rank: blue

Favorite move: hook kick

NARSHA (NAR-SHA)

Narsha is the nicest cobra you'd ever want to meet. Even though she doesn't have any arms or legs, she is one of the best in her Taekwondo class. She always works hard but keeps a smile on her face.

Name means: "flying high"

Belt rank: brown

Favorite move: tail strike

BARON (BAR-ROON)

Baron is the highest rank in his Taekwondo class. He is a great leader; he just doesn't know it yet. He is always willing to help.

Name means: "righteous"

Belt rank: red

Favorite move: palm strike

MASTER TAEKWON LEE is a seventh-degree black belt and master instructor with many years of experience with ATA International—the world's largest martial arts licensing company. He's also the creator of the award-winning interactive children's video series Agent G. He lives in Little Rock, Arkansas.

JEFFREY NODELMAN is a graphic artist, novelist, painter, and award-winning animator who has worked with Walt Disney, Warner Bros., and Nickelodeon. He is a fourth-degree black belt trained in ATA Songahm Taekwondo and a USA-certified ice hockey coach. He lives in Little Rock, Arkansas, with one wife, two children, and three spoiled rescue dogs.

ETHEN BEAVERS is the illustrator of comics for DC Comics, Dark Horse Comics, and IDW Publishing, as well as numerous kids' titles, including the *New York Times* bestselling series NERDS. He lives in central California. Visit ethenbeavers.com.

THANK YOU FOR READING TEAM TAEKWONDO.

WE HOPE YOU ENJOYED IT!

If you would like to redeem **One Free Class** at a participating independently owned and operated ATA-licensed location near you, please visit:

WWW.ATATIGERS.COM/FREECLASS

3 1901 06143 9123

One Free Class offer may vary.